WIZARD OF OZ
ACTIVITY BOOK

David Schimmell

DOVER PUBLICATIONS, INC.
Mineola, New York

Note

The *Wizard of Oz* is a timeless classic loaded with unusual characters facing some difficult situations. After being swept up by a cyclone, poor Dorothy and her little dog, Toto, find themselves in a strange world. After making some new friends, the Scarecrow, Tin Woodman, and Cowardly Lion, Dorothy is faced with many obstacles. In this activity book you will meet some of Dorothy's friends and enemies and go on the journey with her as she tries to get back to Kansas. There are search-a-words, crosswords, connect-the-dots, and more. If you need help with a puzzle you can read the *Wizard of Oz* (available as a Dover reprint). If you want to check your answers, the solutions begin on page 39. And after you're through solving all the puzzles, you can color them any way you choose!

Copyright

Copyright © 2011 by Dover Publications, Inc.
All rights reserved.

Bibliographical Note

Wizard of Oz Activity Book is a new work, first published by Dover Publications, Inc., in 2011.

International Standard Book Number

ISBN-13: 978-0-486-48095-4
ISBN-10: 0-486-48095-X

Manufactured in the United States by LSC Communications
48095X06   2019
www.doverpublications.com

Help Toto make his way through the maze so he can get back into Dorothy's arms.

The cyclone is coming! How many leaves do you see blowing around in this scene? Take a guess before counting them.

>100

Tip: To help keep track while counting, color the leaves in groups of 10, using a different color for each group. After you color 10 leaves the same color, switch to a different color and color 10 more leaves, and so on. Keep coloring in groups until you eventually come to an amount that is less than 10. When that happens, count up how many groups of 10 you colored, multiply that number by 10, and then add the left over leaves to your total.

These hats got all mixed up! Help these characters get their hats back by drawing an arrow from each hat to the person it belongs to.

MUNCHKINS
GLINDA
SCARECROW
KALIDAHS
WINKIES
BOQ
OZ
GAYELETTE
QUELALA
QUADLINGS

```
S  W  G  G  F  J  L  O  N  M  R  V  F  G  J
O  G  A  L  A  L  E  U  Q  J  X  L  H  F  B
D  D  J  Q  K  D  Z  P  B  F  Y  B  R  W  I
S  K  A  L  I  D  A  H  S  K  I  E  E  O  N
S  B  L  G  X  J  J  N  B  M  U  O  M  J  N
J  O  T  H  V  V  K  Q  M  O  B  B  D  S  O
O  Z  P  K  I  I  D  Z  W  K  Q  O  D  Q  S
F  S  C  A  R  E  C  R  O  W  B  Z  A  E  G
N  L  F  D  U  O  S  B  G  C  O  F  I  Z  L
Y  M  U  N  C  H  K  I  N  S  L  K  Y  O  I
Z  J  T  T  K  Q  Q  O  B  J  N  T  I  V  N
Q  W  Y  L  U  T  D  O  N  I  G  Y  S  N  D
D  T  Y  M  L  B  K  H  W  D  A  J  B  J  A
G  A  Y  E  L  E  T  T  E  K  L  X  F  H  Y
R  F  G  S  S  G  N  I  L  D  A  U  Q  Y  T
```

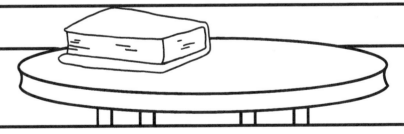

Dorothy has a long journey ahead of her. On her journey, she will
meet or hear of the characters listed in the box on page 4. See if you
can find those characters in the word search puzzle above and circle
them. Make sure you look up, down, across, diagonally, and backwards.

Here you see the Munchkins thanking Dorothy for freeing them
from the Wicked Witch of the East.

Test your drawing skills and finish this drawing so it matches the one on the opposite page.

The Wicked Witch of the West is holding Dorothy, the Cowardly Lion, and the Winkies prisoner. It looks like Dorothy might be in for a lifetime of cleaning pots and kettles, sweeping floors, and keeping the fire fed. See if you can find the 13 objects on the next page hidden within the scene and circle them.

9

A house has fallen on top of the Wicked Witch of the East. Five of the 6 pictures below are the same. Circle the one that is different.

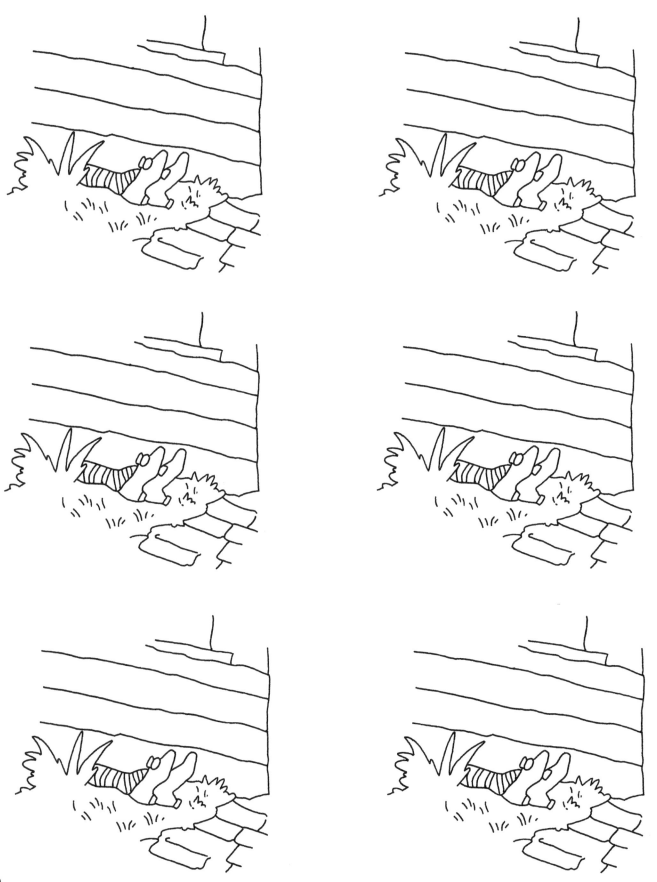

Here are some fiddlers showing their appreciation for Dorothy.
Color this picture any way you like.

In the left column are 3 different characters. In the middle and on the right are unfinished pictures of these characters. See if you can complete these pictures to match the finished ones.

Here are 8 Munchkins. There are only 2 Munchkins that are exactly the same. See if you can find the 2 Munchkins, then circle them.

Help Dorothy find her way through the maze so she can visit the Scarecrow.

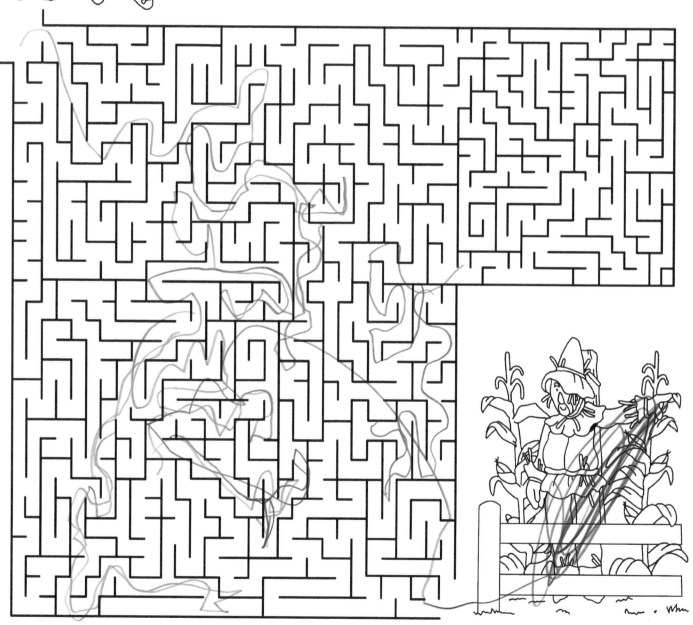

The Scarecrow isn't very good at scaring crows! See if you can count how many crows are in the cornfield. Take a guess before you start counting.

Dorothy is meeting the Tin Woodman for the first time. See if you can find the 8 items below hidden in the picture then circle them.

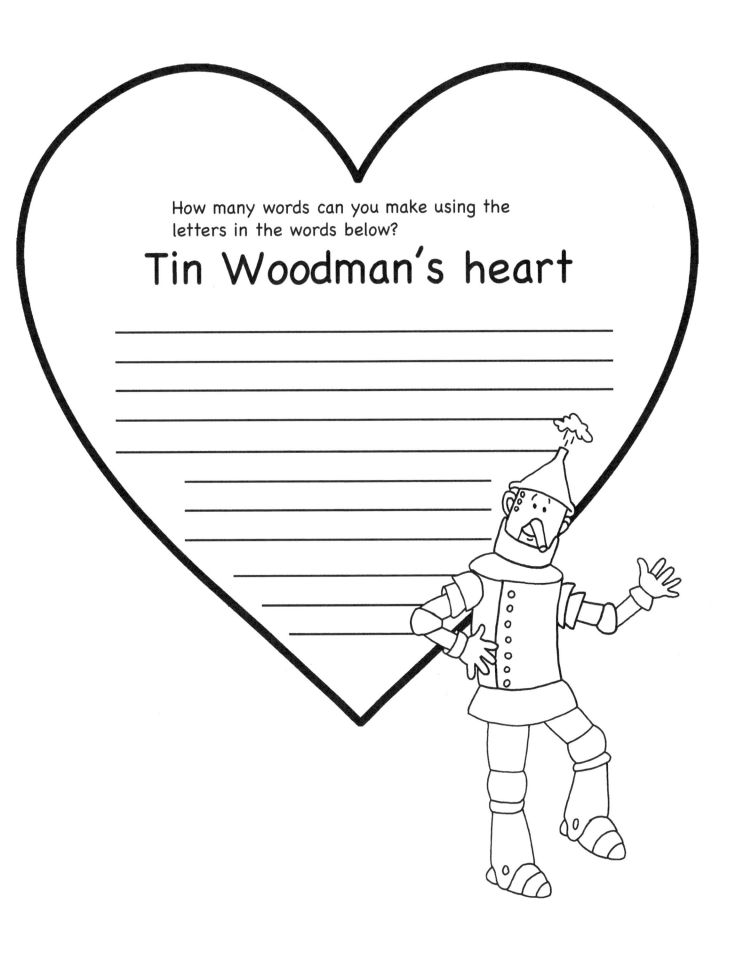

How many words can you make using the letters in the words below?

Tin Woodman's heart

In this scene Dorothy meets the Cowardly Lion while traveling on the yellow brick road.

Here is the same picture, but when you look closely there are 21 changes. See if you can spot the differences, then circle them.

The Wicked Witch of the West has ordered the Winged Monkeys to attack Dorothy and her friends. There are 9 objects above this picture. See if you can find them hidden in the scene and circle them.

The Cowardly Lion is counting sheep because he can't sleep. Take a good look at this picture and see if you can count all the sheep. Try guessing before you start counting.

The Cowardly Lion is trying to get away from the Wicked Witch of the West. It seems that everywhere he turns she is there with her terrifying laugh. Help guide the Cowardly Lion through the maze so he can get back safely to his friends.

Start

Finish

Circle the characters who do not belong in the Wizard of Oz story.

Super Friend

She saved the life of the Cowardly Lion, taught Dorothy how to use the Golden Cap, and gave them directions on how to get to the Emerald City. Who is this "super friend?" To find out, write the letter of the alphabet that comes after the letter shown in the box.

P ☐
T ☐
D ☐
D ☐
M ☐
N ☐
E ☐
S ☐
G ☐
D ☐
L ☐
H ☐
B ☐
D ☐

Help the Scarecrow, Cowardly Lion, and Tin Woodman find their way up the mountain to the home of the Wicked Witch of the West.

Finish

Start

25

Draw what you think surprised Dorothy and her friends.

Complete the crossword puzzle by using the picture clues. Write each word where it belongs in the puzzle. One word has been done for you.

2 across

2 down

1 down

1 across

B R O O M S T I C K

2 down

3 down

3 down

1 across

4 down

1 down

4 down

2 across

Connect the dots from 1 to 100 to see one of the characters in the Wizard of Oz story.

After the death of the Wicked Witch of the West and after Dorothy went back home to Kansas, the Cowardly Lion, Tin Woodman, and Scarecrow went on to live very important lives. To find out their new roles, use the code below.

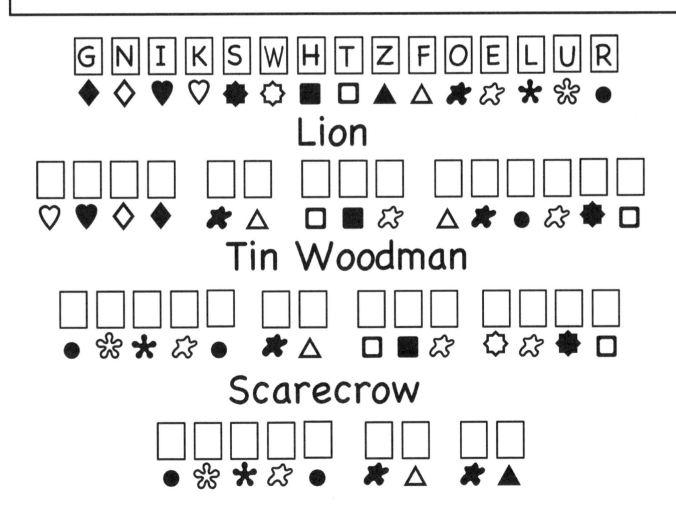

G	N	I	K	S	W	H	T	Z	F	O	E	L	U	R

Lion

Tin Woodman

Scarecrow

See if you can find the words listed in the box in the word search puzzle and circle them. Make sure you look up, down, across, diagonally, and backwards.

```
U C L Y B G N I Y L F P C E J
S T F R T B K G R E E N P T U
T E M E F S V U S I Y N C N S
S K H T K O D U Y O O M T D S
G O L S R S Z K E H P U B D P
E M A I R I D E K C I W V M Z
Z S D S Z E E X N T R W V C L
R W Z W X W P J O I C J A H W
G N I T L E M P M W N S B M A
F K F V K H R F I F T C E E T
U R B I Z V M B D L A W W O E
K L U T R R F H E C S J P S R
R C I U L T I F K D P O C W U
K B M F I M R L B R O O M R G
V J Z F Z K E G Y U U Z E Y U
```

<table>
<tr><td>MELTING</td><td>FLYING</td></tr>
<tr><td>CACKLE</td><td>BROOM</td></tr>
<tr><td>WATER</td><td>SMOKE</td></tr>
<tr><td>MONKEYS</td><td>SISTER</td></tr>
<tr><td>WITCH</td><td>CASTLE</td></tr>
<tr><td>SLIPPERS</td><td>GREEN</td></tr>
<tr><td>WICKED</td><td>FIRE</td></tr>
</table>

Time Line of Events

As requested by the Wizard, Dorothy defeated the Wicked Witch of the West. It was quite a journey. See if you can take the events listed below and put them in the proper order. The first one is done for you.

Dorothy meets the Winkies

Dorothy meets the Scarecrow

Dorothy meets the Good Witch of the North

Dorothy meets the Wicked Witch of the West

Dorothy meets the Tin Woodman

Dorothy meets the Cowardly Lion

Dorothy meets the Wizard

Dorothy meets the Munchkins

Dorothy meets the Queen of the Field Mice

1 Dorothy meets the Good Witch of the North

2 _____

3 _____

4 _____

5 _____

6 _____

7 _____

8 _____

9 _____

See if you can find the words listed in the box in the word search
puzzle and circle them. Make sure you look up, down, across,
diagonally, and backwards.

```
Z  D  A  O  C  V  M  U  M  F  P  Q  R  A  L
K  R  C  P  S  R  J  I  D  W  W  E  V  X  U
B  A  Z  Q  D  D  X  Y  W  J  D  A  J  D  H
V  Z  G  K  L  A  P  Y  P  A  I  N  D  U  A
A  I  P  R  A  Y  S  P  E  X  R  V  D  I  H
Z  W  D  U  R  N  T  L  G  B  Y  O  I  C  A
J  Y  M  L  E  F  O  I  H  U  M  B  U  G  M
Y  T  T  L  M  W  K  O  C  L  Q  R  B  S  O
B  R  T  K  E  R  U  R  L  L  N  F  E  T  E
K  S  Q  B  N  W  H  H  O  L  F  Y  C  T  S
F  L  U  F  R  E  W  O  P  P  A  X  V  H  X
P  H  U  S  P  Z  C  N  G  B  H  B  I  T  W
U  Q  I  L  P  F  H  G  P  B  L  F  Y  D  K
Z  O  I  I  I  X  B  L  H  F  T  U  T  P  X
K  C  R  O  O  K  E  D  A  Y  R  E  P  U  Q
```

WIZARD   OMAHA
LEADER   CROOKED
BALLOON   CITY
EMERALDS SHIFTY
HUMBUG   POWERFUL

In the left column are 3 different characters. In the middle and on the right are unfinished pictures of these characters. See if you can complete these pictures to match the column on the left.

The Wicked Witch of the West is trying to stop Dorothy and her friends. First she sent a pack of great wolves to tear them to pieces, then a great flock of wild crows to peck their eyes out, but nothing could stop them. What will the Wicked Witch send next? Use the code below to find out.

Some of these words belong with Dorothy; others belong with the Wicked Witch. Write the words next to the proper person.

Scarecrow
Kansas
Winkies
Tin Woodman
Great Wolves
Black Bees
Auntie Em
broomstick
Toto
Witch of the East
Uncle Henry
castle
wicked
Cowardly Lion

Take a good look at the silhouettes and draw an arrow pointing to the correct character.

Dorothy never knew she had the power to go back to Kansas all along by wearing the silver shoes. Glinda the Good Witch told Dorothy to click her heels 3 times and say 6 words then she would be home. To find out what Dorothy said, use the code below.

1 = K   4 = A   7 = O
2 = T   5 = M   8 = N
3 = E   6 = H   9 = U

___ ___ ___ ___   ___ ___
 2   4   1   3   5   3

___ ___ ___ ___   ___ ___
 6   7   5   3   2   7

___ ___ ___ ___   ___ ___ !
 4   9   8   2   3   5

Dorothy found out the truth about the Wizard. Read the statements below and check off which ones are true or false.

T F

The silver shoes were once owned by the Wicked Witch of the West. ___ ___

The Queen of the Field Mice once saved the life of the Cowardly Lion. ___ ___

The Tin Woodman was once in love with a Munchkin. ___ ___

Munchkins are originally from Kansas. ___ ___

The Emerald City was the capital of Never-Never Land. ___ ___

Auntie Em lived inside of a crystal ball. ___ ___

Poppies can make people very sleepy. ___ ___

The Cowardly Lion became the King of the Forest after defeating a great spider monster. ___ ___

When Dorothy met the Scarecrow he was just a little over 2 days old. ___ ___

SOLUTIONS

Page 1

There are 115 leaves.

Page 2

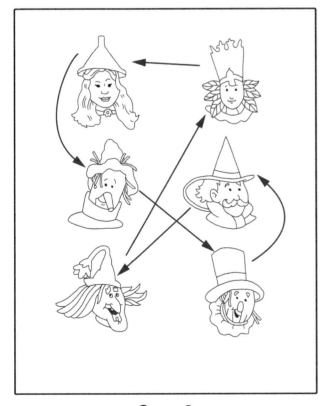

Page 3

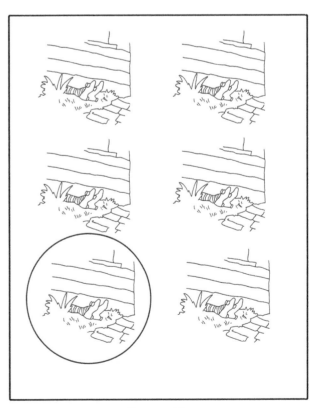

Page 10

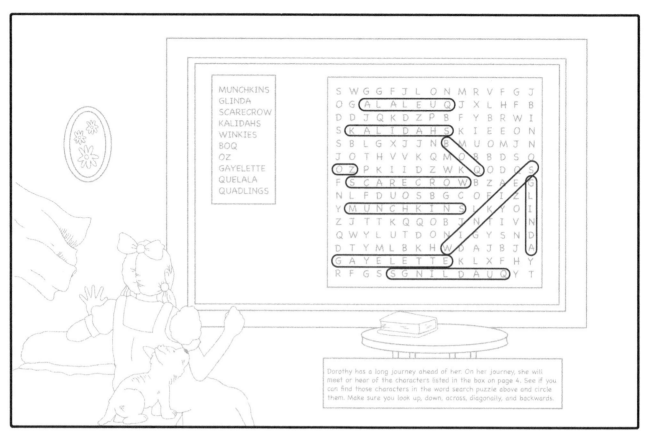

MUNCHKINS
GLINDA
SCARECROW
KALIDAHS
WINKIES
BOQ
OZ
GAYELETTE
QUELALA
QUADLINGS

```
S W G G F J L O N M R V F G J
O G A L A L E U Q J X L H F B
D D J Q K D Z P B F Y B R W I
S K A L I D A H S K I E E O N
S B L G X J J N B M U O M J N
J O T H V V K Q M O R B D S O
O Z P K I I D Z W K Q O D Q S
F S C A R E C R O W B Z A E G
N L F D U O S B G C O F I Z L
Y M U N C H K I N S I K Y O I
Z J T T K Q Q O B J N T I V N
Q W Y L U T D O N I G Y S N D
D T Y M L B K H W O A J B J A
E N G A Y E L E T T E K L X F H Y
R F G S S G N I L D A U Q Y T
```

Dorothy has a long journey ahead of her. On her journey, she will meet or hear of the characters listed in the box on page 4. See if you can find those characters in the word search puzzle above and circle them. Make sure you look up, down, across, diagonally, and backwards.

Pages 4 & 5

The Wicked Witch of the West is holding Dorothy, the Cowardly Lion, and the Winkies prisoner. It looks like Dorothy might be in for a lifetime of cleaning pots and kettles, sweeping floors, and keeping the fire fed. See if you can find the 13 objects on the next page hidden within the scene and circle them.

Pages 8 & 9

Page 13

Page 14

There are 27 crows

Page 15

Page 16

Also, Scarecrow's collar is missing. Tin Man is missing vertical buttons as well as stripes on his right shoe. Lion is missing an ear.

Page 19

Page 20

There are 32 sheep

Page 21

Page 22

Page 23

Super Friend

She saved the life of the Cowardly Lion, taught Dorothy how to use the Golden Cap, and gave them directions on how to get to the Emerald City. Who is this "super friend?" To find out, write the letter of the alphabet that comes after the letter shown in the box.

P	Q
T	U
D	E
D	E
M	N
N	O
E	F
S	T
G	H
D	E
L	M
H	I
B	C
D	E

Page 24

Help the Scarecrow, Cowardly Lion, and Tin Woodman find their way up the mountain to the home of the Wicked Witch of the West.

Finish

Start

Page 25

Page 27

After the death of the Wicked Witch of the West and after Dorothy went back home to Kansas, the Cowardly Lion, Tin Woodman, and Scarecrow went on to live very important lives. To find out their new roles, use the code below.

G N I K S W H T Z F O E L U R
♦ ◇ ♥ ♡ ❀ ◉ ■ □ ▲ △ ♣ ✿ ☆ ✳ ●

Lion

K I N G   O F   T H E   F O R E S T
♡ ♥ ◇ ♦   ✿ △   □ ■ ♡   ✿ ● ✿ ❀ □

Tin Woodman

R U L E R   O F   T H E   W E S T
● ✿ ☆ ✿ ●   ✿ △   □ ■ ✿   ◎ ✿ ❀ □

Scarecrow

R U L E R   O F   O Z
● ✿ ☆ ✿ ●   ✿ △   ✿ ▲

Page 29

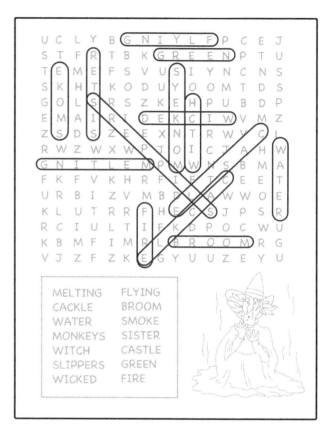

MELTING	FLYING	
CACKLE	BROOM	
WATER	SMOKE	
MONKEYS	SISTER	
WITCH	CASTLE	
SLIPPERS	GREEN	
WICKED	FIRE	

Page 30

Time Line of Events

As requested by the Wizard, Dorothy defeated the Wicked Witch of the West. It was quite a journey. See if you can take the events listed below and put them in the proper order. The first one is done for you.

Dorothy meets the Winkies

Dorothy meets the Scarecrow

Dorothy meets the Good Witch of the North

Dorothy meets the Wicked Witch of the West

Dorothy meets the Tin Woodman

Dorothy meets the Cowardly Lion

Dorothy meets the Wizard

Dorothy meets the Munchkins

Dorothy meets the Queen of the Field Mice

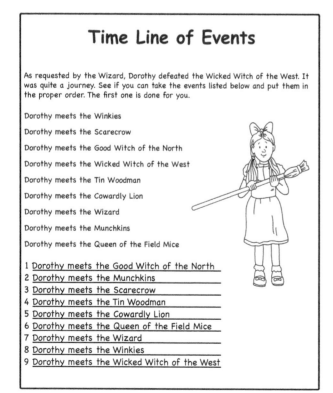

1 Dorothy meets the Good Witch of the North
2 Dorothy meets the Munchkins
3 Dorothy meets the Scarecrow
4 Dorothy meets the Tin Woodman
5 Dorothy meets the Cowardly Lion
6 Dorothy meets the Queen of the Field Mice
7 Dorothy meets the Wizard
8 Dorothy meets the Winkies
9 Dorothy meets the Wicked Witch of the West

Page 31

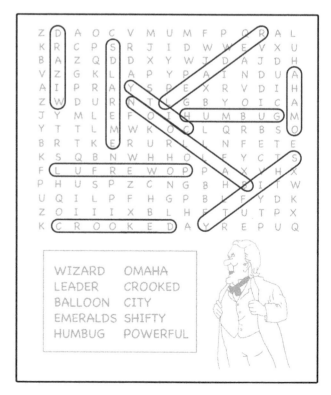

WIZARD	OMAHA
LEADER	CROOKED
BALLOON	CITY
EMERALDS	SHIFTY
HUMBUG	POWERFUL

Page 32

Page 34

Some of these words belong with Dorothy; others belong with the Wicked Witch. Write the words next to the proper person.

Scarecrow
Kansas
Winkies
Tin Woodman
Great Wolves
Black Bees
Auntie Em
broomstick
Toto
Witch of the East
Uncle Henry
castle
wicked
Cowardly Lion

Scarecrow
Kansas
Tin Woodman
Auntie Em
Toto
Uncle Henry
Cowardly Lion

Winkies
Great Wolves
Black Bees
broomstick
Witch of the East
castle
wicked

Page 35

Page 36

1=K 4=A 7=O
2=T 5=M 8=N
3=E 6=H 9=U

T A K E   M E
2 4 1 3   5 3

H O M E   T O
6 7 5 3   2 7

A U N T   E M !
4 9 8 2   3 5

Page 37

45

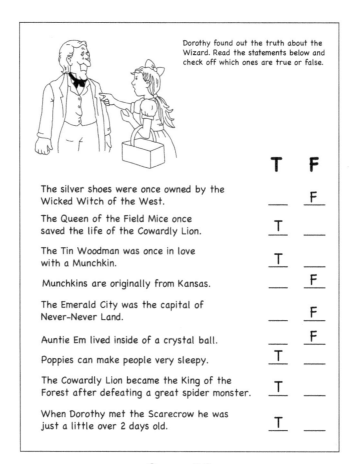

Dorothy found out the truth about the Wizard. Read the statements below and check off which ones are true or false.

	T	F
The silver shoes were once owned by the Wicked Witch of the West.		F
The Queen of the Field Mice once saved the life of the Cowardly Lion.	T	
The Tin Woodman was once in love with a Munchkin.	T	
Munchkins are originally from Kansas.		F
The Emerald City was the capital of Never-Never Land.		F
Auntie Em lived inside of a crystal ball.		F
Poppies can make people very sleepy.	T	
The Cowardly Lion became the King of the Forest after defeating a great spider monster.	T	
When Dorothy met the Scarecrow he was just a little over 2 days old.	T	

Page 38